READ ALL THESE

# NATE THE GREAT DETECTIVE STORIES

AND CONTINUE THE DETECTIVE FUN WITH

# OLIVIA SHARP

*by Marjorie Weinman Sharmat and Mitchell Sharmat
illustrated by Denise Brunkus*

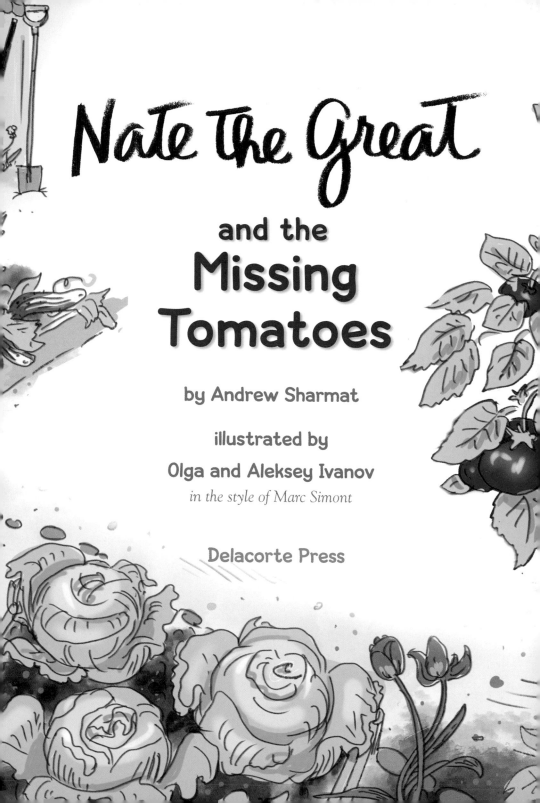

# Nate the Great

## and the
## Missing
## Tomatoes

by Andrew Sharmat

illustrated by

Olga and Aleksey Ivanov

*in the style of Marc Simont*

Delacorte Press

Text copyright © 2022 by Andrew Sharmat
Cover art and interior illustrations copyright © 2022 by Olga and Aleksey Ivanov

All rights reserved. Published in the United States by Delacorte Press, an imprint of Random House Children's Books, a division of Penguin Random House LLC, New York.

New illustrations of Nate the Great, Sludge, Rosamond, Esmeralda, Annie, Claude, and Harry by Olga and Aleksey Ivanov based upon original drawings by Marc Simont.

Delacorte Press is a registered trademark and the colophon is a trademark of Penguin Random House LLC.

Visit us on the Web! rhcbooks.com

Educators and librarians, for a variety of teaching tools, visit us at RHTeachersLibrarians.com

Library of Congress Cataloging-in-Publication Data is available upon request.
ISBN 978-0-593-18087-7 (hardcover) — ISBN 978-0-593-18088-4 (lib. bdg.) — ISBN 978-0-593-18089-1 (ebook)

The text of this book is set in 17-point Goudy.
Interior design by Sylvia Bi

Printed in the United States of America
10 9 8 7 6 5 4 3 2 1
First Edition

*To Lisa, my favorite gardener*

## Chapter One

# Making a Meal, Making a Mess

I, Nate the Great, am a detective.
My dog, Sludge, is also a detective.
When I am not on a case, I like to cook.
I like to cook pancakes in the kitchen.
When Sludge is not on a case,
he likes to dig.
He likes to dig up bones in the yard.
This morning we made our favorite
breakfast of pancakes and bones.
We also made a big mess.

I had knocked pancake batter on the floor
and was now cleaning up.
Sludge had dug up half of the yard.
He was not cleaning up.
Dogs don't like to clean.

The phone rang.
It was Rosamond.

"Nate the Great, I need your help!" she
shouted. "I've been growing tomatoes in my
garden, and some of them are missing."
I, Nate the Great, do not like tomatoes.
If I were missing tomatoes,
I would not look for them.
But this was a new case.
"We will be right over," I said.
I looked at the mess in the kitchen and
the bigger mess in the yard.
"We will be over in a little while," I said.
I finished cleaning up the kitchen.

Then I wrote a note to my mother.

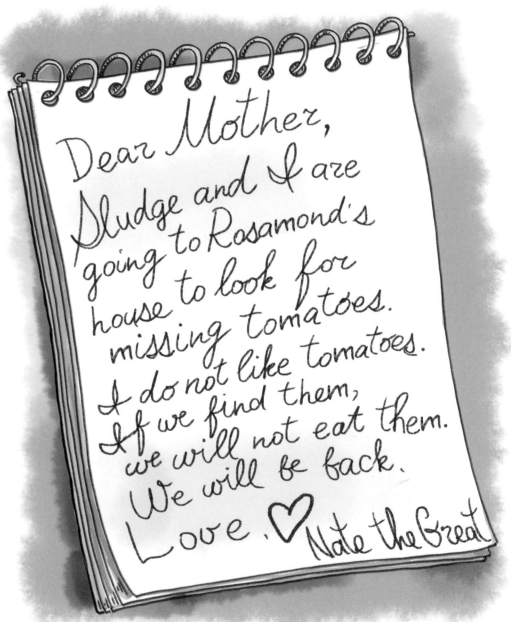

Dear Mother,
Sludge and I are
going to Rosamond's
house to look for
missing tomatoes.
I do not like tomatoes.
If we find them,
we will not eat them.
We will be back.
Love, Nate the Great

## Chapter Two

# The Garden of Hexes and Tomatoes

Rosamond is very strange.
Strange things are always happening
at her house.
Today things were stranger than usual.
Rosamond has four black cats: Big Hex,
Little Hex, Super Hex, and Plain Hex.
All four cats were wearing helmets.
Rosamond was wearing a helmet too.
She was also holding a shovel.

Rosamond and the Hexes were digging a
trench around a small vegetable garden.
Rosamond was digging with her shovel.
The Hexes were digging with their claws.

"Welcome to my construction zone,"
she said.
"Why are you digging a trench?" I asked.
"This isn't a trench. It's a moat."
Sludge and I stared at Rosamond.

"A moat to protect my tomato garden,"
she said.

"How did you get your cats to help?" I asked.

"I plan to stock my moat with fish,"
Rosamond said.

"That would do it," I said.

"And maybe a crocodile," she added.

Rosamond's cats stopped digging.

"Someone is taking my tomatoes.

"Look at all these bare vines," Rosamond said. "I think it might be Esmeralda." "Esmeralda wouldn't take your tomatoes," I said. "Esmeralda is smart, honest, and kind." "True," Rosamond said. "But she, Finley, Oliver, Annie, and I are competing to grow the best organic garden. Claude was in the contest, but his plants dried up." "Dried up?" I asked.

"Plants grow better when you water them," Rosamond said.

"When is the contest?" I asked.

"In three days," Rosamond said.

"The winner gets a ribbon, and an article and photo in the newspaper.

The judge is Uncle Ned from Uncle Ned's Day and Night Diner. My tomatoes are huge and juicy, so I will certainly win."
"Esmeralda would never take your tomatoes," I said.

"The winner also gets a month's supply
of Uncle Ned's famous apple pies,"
Rosamond told me. "Plus three cases of
his homemade ice cream."

"Esmeralda would never take your
tomatoes," I repeated.
"And Ned's amazing pancakes," she added.
"All you can eat."

"His pancakes are pretty good," I said.
"Maybe Esmeralda did take your—"
Sludge looked at me.
"Sorry," I said. "I, Nate the Great, say your tomatoes were eaten by an animal. Maybe a rabbit, or a raccoon, or a squirrel, or a deer. We will search your garden for clues."

## Chapter Three
# The Tomatoes of Kitty-Cat Farms

I noticed a large sign in the ground in Rosamond's garden.
The sign read:

KITTY-CAT FARMS
WORLD'S GREATEST
GIANT TOMATOES
YOU PICK 'EM—JUST
25¢

"You're selling your tomatoes?" I asked.
"If you sell them all, you'll lose the contest."
"But I'll be rich," said Rosamond. "So it will
be worth it."

"How many have you sold?" I asked.
"I'm still waiting for my first sale," she said.
Sludge sniffed a tomato.
Then we walked around the garden.
It had rained two nights ago, and
the ground was still muddy.
I took out my magnifying glass and searched
the ground for clues.

I searched and searched.
Sludge sniffed and sniffed.
We found pawprints. Many different kinds.
We found footprints. Two different kinds.

Rosamond's garden was popular with
animals and people.
But mostly with animals.
Suddenly, I spotted a small tray.
There were two quarters on it.
"You found
my tray,"
Rosamond said.
"Yes, and two
quarters," I said.
"Those quarters
are my first
sale!" Rosamond
shouted.

"And those quarters are my first clues,"
I said.
"I think the other clues are with Esmeralda,"
Rosamond said.
"Why are you so sure?" I asked.
"Because Esmeralda loves Uncle Ned's.

"She told me that it's her favorite diner and that she was going to work hard to win the contest," Rosamond said.

I thought about the free pancakes at Ned's. Free pancakes from Uncle Ned's might be hard to resist.

Maybe Esmeralda had taken the tomatoes.

It was time to pay her a visit.

## Chapter Four

# Another Garden, Another Quarter

Esmeralda's vegetable garden was different from Rosamond's.

First, there was no moat. Second, it had a lot more than just tomatoes.

Esmeralda was growing lettuce and spinach, cucumbers and carrots, squash and radishes, snow peas and potatoes, chard and turnips, watermelons and honeydew.

There were even giant stalks of corn.

And lots of huge red tomatoes.

I, Nate the Great, knew there was
no chance that Esmeralda was going
to lose the contest.
There was also no chance that she had
taken any tomatoes.
She didn't need to.

"Hello, Nate the Great," Esmeralda said.
"Are you here to look for Rosamond's
tomatoes?"
"How did you know?" I asked.
"She asked me if I took them,"
Esmeralda said.
"You don't need them. Your garden is
amazing. You will win the contest."
"Everything here is organic," Esmeralda
said. "All-natural, very healthy.

I'm going to give some of my veggies to
the local food bank. Some people don't
have enough food to eat. I want to help.

I also want to help you find Rosamond's
tomatoes."
Esmeralda thinks she is a detective.
But I already have Sludge, the world's
greatest detective's assistant.
He was digging in the mud.
He looked up at me and wagged his tail.
Sludge had found something.

It was a quarter.
Another clue, I thought.
"Are you missing any tomatoes?" I asked.

Esmeralda carefully looked at her
tomato plants.
"Yes," she said. "There is one big
tomato missing."
"Rosamond
is selling her
tomatoes for
one quarter
each," I said.
"Are you
selling your
tomatoes?"
"No,"
Esmeralda
said. "But if you would like to buy one—"
"No, thanks," I said. "I like pancakes.
And Sludge likes bones.
And we both like clues."
I thought about the quarters.

It was strange that there would be
quarters left in both gardens.
"These quarters are clues," I said. "If I can
figure out the connection between the
quarters, I will solve this case."
I decided to visit Annie's house.
Annie was also in the contest.
Maybe someone had left a quarter
in her garden.

## Chapter Five
# Fang's Big Mess

Sludge and I rushed to Annie's house.
The good news was that Annie was home.
The bad news was that her dog, Fang,
was home too.
Fang has big, shiny, sharp teeth.
Today his teeth looked bigger, shinier, and
sharper than usual.

Fang must be a superstar at the dentist's office.

"Hello, Annie," I said. "Sludge and I are on a case. Rosamond is missing tomatoes from her garden. She thinks that someone took them."

"Well, she's lucky that she still has a garden," Annie said. "Mine has been completely destroyed."

"Destroyed?" I asked.

"Yes," Annie said. "Destroyed, trashed, smashed, wrecked, vaporized."

"Vaporized?" I asked.

"Well, ruined," Annie said.
"Come outside. I'll show you."
We all walked outside to look
at Annie's garden.
The area was a mess.

The ground was a muddy mess.

"When did this happen?" I asked.

"Sometime this morning," Annie said.

"I went to buy more seeds. When I came home, the garden was dug up. Who would do this?" she asked.

Then Annie pointed to a small, shiny object in the mud pile.

"Look!" she shouted. "There's a quarter stuck in the mud!"

The case was getting stranger.

Rosamond was missing many tomatoes, but had two quarters placed in her garden.

Esmeralda had only one tomato missing and only one quarter.

Annie's garden had been destroyed, and she also had one quarter.

Clearly, Annie had gotten the worst of it.
I, Nate the Great, was now confused.
What did all these quarters mean?
And who would steal tomatoes and
destroy a garden?
"What are you thinking about?"
Annie asked.
"Right now, I'm thinking about eating
pancakes," I said. "Fluffy dough, butter,
syrup, a glass of milk. Yum."
Annie looked angry.
"But first, we will search your garden,"
I said.
I took out my magnifying glass and looked
in the mud.

I saw claw marks and white hair
scattered about.
I now knew who had destroyed
Annie's garden.
I looked at Fang.
Fang growled at me.
I decided that it might be safer if I was
far away when I reported the results
of my search to Annie.
"I, Nate the Great, believe I know who
dug up your garden," I said.
"But I need to check some clues first.
I will call you later."

## Chapter Six

# Come for the Pancakes, Stay for the Clues

Sludge and I were headed home
I needed to think about the clues.
On the way, we passed Uncle Ned's Day and
Night Diner.

Sludge was sniffing.

I was sniffing.

We both smelled food coming from
Ned's diner.

Sludge stopped and sat in front of the door.

"Let's go," I said.

But Sludge wouldn't move.

"Okay," I said. "We can eat here."
Sludge wagged his tail.
Ned's was busy. I sat in the only open seat
at the counter.
"Are you here on a case?" Ned asked.
"I am here for pancakes," I said. "I'm on a
case, and pancakes help me think."
"And a bone for Sludge?" Ned asked.
"Yes," I said. "He needs to think too."
Sludge wagged his tail again.

I waited for the pancakes to cook.
And I thought about the quarters and the
missing tomatoes.
Nothing made sense.
Then Sludge turned to the front
of the diner.

He was pointing with his nose.
The window was open.
On the windowsill was a row of
giant tomatoes.

A row of giant tomatoes with faces
painted on them.
Sludge must have smelled them when
we were outside.
"Uncle Ned," I said. "Where did those
tomatoes with the faces come from?"
"You might not believe this," he said.
"They're a gift from Claude. He left them
here this morning."
"A gift from Claude?" I asked.
"A gift from Claude," he repeated.
"He was in the gardening contest, but
his plants dried up."
"They grow better when you water them,"
I said.
"Claude painted the faces of my family
on the tomatoes," Ned said. "He gave up
gardening to become a tomato artist. He
wants to display his tomatoes here so that
all my diners can see his work."

Uncle Ned pointed at each tomato.

"This one is me.

Then there's my
wife, Evelyn;

my daughter, Rhoda;

and my son, Joe.

"Nice, aren't they?"

I stared at the tomatoes. Sludge stared at the tomatoes.

"Those don't look anything like your family," I said.

"Well, they are tomatoes, so that's not a surprise," Uncle Ned said.

Next to the tomatoes was a hot dog. The hot dog had been dressed up with glued-on cardboard ears, four short cardboard legs, and a stumpy cardboard tail.

"We also have a dachshund named Blitz,"
Ned said.
"Did Claude paint your tomatoes,
or did he bring his own?" I asked.
"He brought his own," Uncle Ned said.
"The pancakes will have to wait," I said.
"We have to find Claude!"

## Chapter Seven
# The Tomato Artist

Sludge and I raced to Claude's house.
We were about to solve the mystery.
Four tomato faces at Ned's and four quarters
left in vegetable gardens. It all added up.
I, Nate the Great, knew that Claude had
taken the tomatoes.
I knew that he had used the tomatoes to
make a gift for Uncle Ned.

I knew that he had left quarters
at each garden.

I rang the doorbell, and Claude answered.
"Hello, Nate the Great," he said.
"Are you here for my tomato artwork?"
"No," I said.
"Good," Claude said. "Because I'm out of
tomatoes. But I can paint your face on any
kind of fruit. Oranges, apples, kumquats."
"Kumquats?" I asked.

"Yes," Claude said. "I could paint your face on a kumquat with a detective's hat on top. Would Sludge like to be painted on a banana?"

Sludge gave a disapproving glance.

"I think I'll ask the questions," I said. "Did you take tomatoes from Esmeralda, Annie, and Rosamond?"

"Yes," Claude said. "My tomatoes dried up.

I found out that they grow better when you water them."

"Did you leave a quarter at Esmeralda's garden?" I asked.

"Yes," he said.

"Did you leave a quarter at Annie's garden?"

"Yes," he said again.

"Did you leave two quarters
at Rosamond's garden?"

"Just one," he said. "I only bought one
tomato from each garden. When I saw that
Rosamond was selling her tomatoes,
I decided to buy one at each garden. I didn't
want anyone to run out of tomatoes."
"That's very nice of you," I said. "But I
found two quarters at Rosamond's, and you

gave four tomatoes with faces to Uncle Ned. Where did you get the fourth tomato?"

"Oliver sold me the other tomato," said Claude.

"Oliver the Follower?" I asked.

"Yes," Claude said. "I thought he was in the contest, so I went to his house to buy my last tomato. Turns out that he quit the contest too. But I got lucky. Oliver has a whole bunch of tomatoes. He sold me two for a quarter. One to eat and one for my gift to Uncle Ned."

"Did he say where he got the tomatoes?"

"I didn't ask," Claude said.

Interesting, I thought. Oliver had dropped out of the contest.

But he had extra tomatoes, and Rosamond was missing tomatoes.

Could there be a connection? It was time to find out.

## Chapter Eight
## A Full Sack

W hen we reached Oliver's house,
I rang the doorbell.
There was no answer.
Then I turned around and got a surprise.

Oliver was standing behind me.
"I followed you from Claude's house,"
he said.
"What were you doing there?"
Oliver likes to follow people.
He might make a good detective's assistant.
Just like Esmeralda.
"I'm looking for Rosamond's missing
tomatoes," I said.
"Missing?" Oliver said. "That's too bad.

Rosamond's tomatoes are
yummy. I keep them in
a sack in my refrigerator.
Would you like a few?"
"You have Rosamond's
tomatoes?" I asked.
"I do have some,"
Oliver said.
"So you stole them?"
I asked.

"I would never steal tomatoes," Oliver said.
"I bought them. They're really juicy and
huge. I got a sackful of tomatoes for
just a quarter!"

"A sackful?" I said. "They're a quarter *each*."

Oliver looked at me. "Each?" he said.
"That's not what the sign says."

I tried to remember. I thought about
what I had read.

KITTY-CAT FARMS
WORLD'S GREATEST
GIANT TOMATOES
YOU PICK 'EM—JUST
25¢

It didn't say 25 cents *each*.

Oliver wasn't a thief.

Oliver was a smart shopper!

"So how did you know that Rosamond was selling her tomatoes?" I asked.

"I was following Claude that day," Oliver said. "I saw him pick a tomato at Rosamond's garden. When I saw the sign and how cheap they were, I couldn't resist.

"I had a sack with me. So I filled it. I got a sackful of tomatoes. Claude got two tomatoes. Rosamond got a quarter from me, and I got a quarter from Claude."

"Everyone wins," I said. "And I win, because my case is now solved."

Chapter Nine
# The Catnap Inn

The case and the contest were over.
Esmeralda took first place.
I was not surprised that Esmeralda won.

Esmeralda, Finley, Annie, Claude,
and Oliver were not surprised
that Esmeralda won.
Sludge was not surprised either.
Rosamond was very surprised.
She was not happy.
I went to her house a week after the contest
to check on her garden and moat.
The garden was gone. A small pond
was in its place.

"You gave up on the garden?" I asked.
"That garden was last week. I'm on to better
things," Rosamond said. "Even though I
should have won the contest, I've decided
to stick with doing what I know best."
"Digging a crocodile pond?" I asked.
"This isn't a crocodile pond," Rosamond
said. "It's a fishpond for my soon-to-be
cat hotel."

"Cat hotel?" I said.

"Welcome to the Catnap Inn. It's the best idea I've ever had. Every cat will want to stay here. We'll have cat dining rooms, cat scratching posts, gold-plated litter boxes, and a bird-watching area."

"Did any birds sign up to be watched by cats?" I said.

"We're having trouble with that," Rosamond said.

"I like the cat hotel idea. Maybe Sludge and I could open a dog hotel. We'll call it the Puppy Plaza Hotel.

"It'll have dog dining rooms,

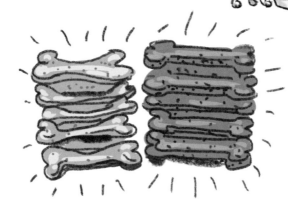

a boneyard,

gold-plated litter boxes,

and a cat-watching area."

"Gold-plated litter boxes at a dog hotel?"
Rosamond asked. "Why?"

"To bring the cats to the cat-watching area,"
I said.

"I don't think I like that idea,"
Rosamond said.

"And the best part will be a special
pancake kitchen," I added.

"For the dogs?" Rosamond asked.

"For me," I said.

I thought for a moment.
Sludge and I hadn't had lunch.

We said goodbye to Rosamond and
started to walk home.
"Maybe I'll just build the pancake kitchen
and forget the hotel," I said to Sludge.
"I'll call it Nate and Sludge's Pancake
Kitchen and Bone Bistro."
Sludge wagged his tail.

"I'll cook the pancakes, and you can be in charge of giving out bones. That means I've got to practice cooking pancakes. And you've got to practice digging more holes. The kitchen and yard are going to be a mess all over again."

Sludge wagged his tail faster than ever.